Where's Sancho?
II

Don Quiett

Making Will: A One Act Play

Inquires concerning all rights should be sent to P.O. Box 271,
Fuquay–Varina, North Carolina 27526

Published by Modern Aesthete

Cover artwork by Don Quiett
Cover design by Cari Corbett

Printed in the United States of America

First Edition

ISBN: 978-0-6151-6494-6

To my heroes and family

Acknowledgements

I would like to thank the Will Rogers Memorial for its wealth of information and willingness to share it. I again thank some modern writers whose insights continually affect my writing. These are: David Sirota, Joe Conason, Norman Solomon, Mark Miller and Robert Kennedy, Jr.

Note

It's nearly impossible to write as Will Rogers spoke. Therefore, I made up some conventions with the hope that they help the reading of Rogers' imitation. Granted, actors and directors will have their own research means to reproduce Rogers' stage demeanor. However, since most readers are probably unfamiliar with him, I felt this exercise may enhance a reading experience. It would be best to hear Rogers first hand and thus, be able to ignore my effort, forming your own mental picture. Tapes/DVDs or cassettes/CDs of Will Rogers can be obtained from Will Rogers Memorial, Claremore, Oklahoma (918–341–0719). Also, brief examples of Rogers speaking can be heard at websites like Wikipedia and Harpers Audio.

When you see the following coming in the dialogue, read as:
> *(ha–ha–ha)* imagine Rogers starting to laugh, 3–4 words before the symbol appears and continuing for 3-4 words after the symbol.
> *(hee–hee–hee)* imagine Rogers giggling as talks, 3–4 words before and after the symbol.
> *(ha–ah–ha–ah)* imagine snickering as talks, 3–4 words before and after symbol.
> *(ah–ah)* read as is, Rogers used as a way to heighten expectation or to suggest a punch line coming.

Finally, Rogers raised his voice as an exclamation point to make the point he wished.

Biographical Sketch of Will Rogers

(1879–1935)

Will Rogers was more than an entertainer, even though he was a comic, movie actor, in the Ziegfeld Follies, pundit, commentator, news columnist and writer. The world had never seen his likes, nor probably will again. He had the uncanny ability to say harsh, pointed, needed –to–be–said–things, yet few, if any, took offense. He was America's conscience and at a time (1920–30's) it needed one, or at least, needed to recognize it had one. With his quiet, "aw–shucks" demeanor, he could say facts in a way making people think, such that their common sense, reason, justness had a chance to bloom, no matter how remote.

Although his life was short, it was not uneventful. Number 11384 on the official Cherokee rolls, in Oklahoma, was indeed Willie, as he was known. Mixed in with his Cherokee ancestors were also Irish, Welsh, English and either German or Dutch. A true American.

After some secondary schooling, he desired to visit Argentina to see gauchos, even though he was poor. The quest begins. He ends up working his way to South Africa via England! Here, he breaks horses for the British Army and drives cattle to earn money to continue his travels. Luckily, a Wild West Show shows up, he joins up and he starts a roping act. The troupe visits Australia, where he joins a circus which journeys to New Zealand and elsewhere. After three years, he again reaches U.S. shores, while never making it to Argentina.

From that point, his life's a whirlwind going from another Wild West Show at the St Louis World's Fair to vaudeville to New York City to, eventually, Ziegfeld Follies, becoming their greatest star.

Then he began writing books like The Cowboy Philosopher on the Peace Conference and weekly news op–ed essays. Travel was always on his mind as well, especially as air travel became more feasible. On a trip to Europe, Rogers declared himself "a self–appointed unofficial ambassador" and as such published reports for President Coolidge in the <u>Saturday Evening Post</u>. These later become a book: <u>Letters of a Self–Made Diplomat to His President</u>.

In 1928, as the Great Depression loomed, he was the master of ceremonies for the first national radio coast to coast hook–up. Millions in the radio audience learned to trust and believe this cowboy philosopher. He had people laughing at other's shortcomings, but all the while these same listeners contemplated their own faults, as well. The balance, proportion and the milk of human kindness of Will Rogers made these discourses flow, positively. Oh, by the way, he also acted in and/or produced movies, which only enhanced his down home stature. The result was <u>Life</u> magazine declaring Rogers: "Unofficial President of the United States." Then, there was more writing, radio and movies until his death in a plane crash in Alaska, in 1935.

This brief biography could be expanded with more of his political posturings and quips, but what seems important is to attempt to derive what made Will Rogers an icon. One should probably start with the fact he was one of us – a common man, or as he was referred to, "typically American." Or maybe it was his "gather–around–the–potbellied–stove–philosopher" demeanor that made his words ring with truth. Or maybe it was the twinkle in his eyes, an infectious grin, his Oklahoma drawl and gum chewing, or that he did not preach or lecture in the accepted way. Or maybe his genius for easing tension made him trustworthy. Or maybe it was his gift to endlessly laugh at himself that made people laugh at themselves. Or maybe his unstuffing of stuffed shirts in a way that they loved it, is a clue. He rejected stuffiness.

Or maybe his appeal was his lack of being intrigued with the put–down. We are far into the era of sick humor. We applaud bold insult. And as our laughter has grown more vicious, our inclination is to go for the throat. Rogers would have none of this. He would have unstuffed us.

Yet, one can not overlook his craft. He created a role for himself in the grand human scene, and played it perfectly. To quote Lloyd Jones, <u>The Tulsa Tribune</u>, "His affected naiveté covered a shrewd mind and a calculating eye. Little that was incongruous or ridiculous escaped him. But he sugarcoated his pill with spurious illiteracy and grammatical gaffes. It was art."

Will Rogers became more than an actor portraying the conscience of America; he actually became it. That plane crash took more than a man from America, and we need whatever it was back, especially in these turbulent times. Common sense, reason, soul, whatever, we need a new Will Rogers. Making Will, a new one, will not be easy, but is desperately cried out for today.[1]

---

[1] Biography information was uncovered at the Will Rogers Memorial in Claremore, Oklahoma (918–341–0719) and from two books: The Best of Will Rogers by Brian Sterling and Letters of a Self–Made Diplomat by Will Rogers with preface by Jenkin Lloyd Jones.

MAKING WILL

by

Don Quiett

(One Act Play)

SETTING

A one room bachelor apartment in a high rise; occupied by two males, both single. Room is junky and in disarray, with minimal furniture. In other words, stereotypical for lay–abouts who are potentially upwardly mobile, restless and anticonformist. Furniture: pre–junkyard, flea market stuff. Setting is in downtown Raleigh, N.C. Scene opens with curtain going up on main characters lounging around with one reading a comic book and the other a newspaper.

CHARACTERS

George – Late twenty–something northerner from Pennsylvania. Writer with nothing to show for efforts except rejection slips. Still dreams. Supports himself by working in a slaughter house at minimum wage.

Tom – Fifty–something, southerner from North Carolina. Textile worker in youth, but after Vietnam could not hold a job, due to medical problems. Dreams too, aspires to be an actor. George and Tom met in a summer theater symposium at their local community center.

MBS 1 and 2 – Men in black suits. Dressed as FBI SWAT team; stern, unyielding, serious and macho government law enforcers.

CURTAIN RISES

GEORGE
(*Throws newspaper down and jumps up*) Damn. That's what I'll do!

TOM
What?

GEORGE

Why didn't this idea bubble up before? Destiny! (*Stares heavenly*)

TOM

Yeah. (*Keeps reading*) Danger Mouse is in trouble now. (*Points at comics*)

GEORGE

My calling, that's it!

TOM

Oh God. Weren't fired, were you?

GEORGE

Eat it!

TOM

Old fart? Is that the calling? Make a good one.

GEORGE

Past do. Past do. Right. Humm. (*Pacing, hand on forehead*)

TOM

About time you did something – Creative. Fat old fart's good as any life calling. – – – At least for you.

GEORGE

(*Ignoring Tom*) Cunning it is.

TOM

What? (*Puts down the comic*) This oughta to be good.

GEORGE

Yep.

TOM

Come on then. Give. I'm all tingly with that – uh, uh anticipation stuff. (*Laughs*)

GEORGE

Wait, I gotta think this out.

TOM

Sure. What?

GEORGE

Will Rogers! That's what! Will rides again! (*Jumps with joy*)

TOM

You gotta watch out for those bends, I hear. And going too fast.

GEORGE

I'll be the new one! (*Paces anxiously*)

TOM

(*Laughing*) Whoo–ooo. Whooo–ooo–. Whoo–ooo. Hey man, (*Whispers, acting like serious but not*) I saw it too! Zap, just entered your body. Willie's ghost. He was kind of purple, huh?

GEORGE

Shut up.

TOM

Does it feel different?

GEORGE

No. No. No. I'll be the New–Age Will Rogers.

TOM

I'll bite. How?

GEORGE

He mostly read newspapers. (*Holds up what he was reading*) For an act, to critique Congress and junk.

TOM

On street corners? You'll do this?

GEORGE

(*Preaching*) "Power is in the hand of too few people, therefore they need <u>watched</u>(!) – closely." No one does it today. (*Stands up, expands chest with arms out*) So, <u>me</u> – Will! (*Yells*)

TOM

(*Calmly*) You're going to read the newspaper and recite C–SPAN telecasts for a new life – living? Do I get this right? Don't we have enough talking heads? That say nothing?

GEORGE

No, no. We need an act. To voice the people's needs, wants. And not nothing.

TOM

Aaah, thought there was a catch. An act.

GEORGE

Think outside the box, Tom. Follow our imaginations. This has potential.

TOM

<u>Me</u>, I'm gonna outsource myself. Mandarin's – the future.

GEORGE

(*Blows out breath*) Doubt if community college Mandarin will suffice.

TOM

Yea, you watch!

GEORGE

Tom, Tom, Tommy. That textile job <u>is</u> gone. What could you make in China anyway – what 50 cents, per hour? No, sorry, per day! A good day.

TOM

Yea, but I'll live like a millionaire on that 50 cents I'm told.

GEORGE

Come on, we're mates. Southerner and Yankee. Maybe it's not too late to heal the Civil War wounds.

TOM

Wanna bet? What's this – mates? We're not Aussies or Brits.

GEORGE

But we're mates all the same. A team. <u>Will's team</u>!

TOM

Where's the beef thing? Money? Christ, you're getting weird.

GEORGE

Details! That comes later. Willie R. read the newspaper for his act. I can do that! He could do it. I can do it. Bingo!

TOM

Bingo, shit.

GEORGE

OK, I'll be new age. Carry a T.V. around and comment as I watch C–SPAN. (*Pretends to carry a portable T.V.*) Wait, listen to this radio tape we got at his museum.

Tape plays briefly

TOM

This is a crock. Why would we do this? Hell, nobody even knows Rogers today. Take the $5.50 per hour from your slaughterhouse job and be happy.

GEORGE

Happy! Happy! A modern–day slave is all I am. That's minimum wage. Don't want to be a loser all your life, do you?

TOM

Aaah, don't think so. – If a choice.

GEORGE

Well, let's not be losers in a big way. Besides, our country, the common people, are crying out for us.

TOM

Oh, no. Country called once. Why I'm here. Where's the country now? So, no! No! No!

GEORGE

You'll see. Trust me.

TOM

Heard that before, too. Being all you can be. Shit.

GEORGE

So, the VA has problems. That's not the people's fault. The people need a voice. Us!

TOM

Like hell. Thought that's what elections were for – and you see where that got us. They can keep their voice.

GEORGE

Stop it, Tom. You know elections are big business, and today, have nothing to do with 'the people.' That's what we'll change. Like Will did. So, teach me some OKLie–HOMIE drawl – to sound like Will.

TOM

They don't have a drawl, just country. Besides, I'm Southern.

GEORGE

Same thing, but OK – OK. I should speak – slooowwlly and shhhlllyyy theeennn. Stretched out! Right?

TOM

You can't ride a horse anyway. Or lasso.

GEORGE

Huh? – don't get it.

TOM

Wait! I'll get you started. A poem. About the color codes that make us seee–curree. (*Said slowly with emphasis*)
>First comes yellow,
>To make me mellow.
>Orange is a watch–outer,
>To make me stouter.
>But when we have red,

We are dead.

                    GEORGE
That's not what Will did. Poems. You better stick to
your day job. Wait, let me get that tape again.

                    TOM
(*After starts playing tape again*) Cut my army benefits off
today.

                    GEORGE
Now, do you get how he – what? Huh? (*Turns tape off*)

                    TOM
Yep, VA letter said I'm cured. Traumatic stress, PTSD, is
just good old combat fatigue again and not worthy of
benefits. Patton rolls back in his grave.

                    GEORGE
Bugger.

                    TOM
Budget cut priority. So much for <u>my</u> country.

                    GEORGE
That's the point! Rogers wouldn't let that pass. Nor, I
bet, would the people. God, this idea gets bigger by the
minute.

                    TOM
Think about it – Nixon, Reagan, Clinton, Bush, Jr. –
have no idea what it's like – video game to them.

                    GEORGE
We oughta put that in the act.

TOM

What act? (*Tom coughs, and prepares himself to speak*)
> Ta taaa –
> I don't go to war,
> But I know more.
> To fight is right by golly gee,
> As long as it's not me.

GEORGE

Right idea, wrong pew. Will didn't do poems. (*George jumps up and snaps his fingers*) We need props! (*Runs to closet and pulls out an old cowboy outfit*) What about these, from my youth?

TOM

What? A fake lasso, frozen in a loop, and a too small cowboy hat and shirt? (*Futzes with lasso*)

GEORGE

Yea, yea! (*Sticks small hat on head, fumbles with shirt with only one arm getting in and whizzes lasso around*) Give me that paper I was reading. Here! Here! How about this? (*Reads, swings lasso and always seems on verge of laughing.*) Ahh – (*hee – hee – hee*). Yep, by golly, says here – yes it does a –ah–ah it says the Pres–e–dent – our boss – (*hee –hee –hee*). Our boss, yea, – well anyway, back to the story – know what I mean, (*Mumbles*) anyway says our occupation in Iraq is not an occupation. It's freedom. Yea, don't that beat all now? Tickles me to death – *(ha– ha –ha)* them guys is smart. Need a new dictionary, though.

TOM

That's funny? Huh? (*Doesn't laugh*)

GEORGE

Yea, think about it! We couldn't make this stuff up!

Will's point! Like saying: our oranges are not oranges.
They're apples.

TOM

Still not funny.

GEORGE

That's why we're a team. Mates. <u>We'll</u> make it funny.
(*Pause*) Eventually.

TOM

Is that a pun or something? Will? <u>We'll</u>?

GEORGE

(*Ignores*) Read the paper in the bar, pub, the other night
and everyone cracked up. Thought I was drunk and
making it up. I couldn't.

TOM

That doesn't count. <u>Drunks</u> – would laugh at anything,
especially if you were buying.

GEORGE

(*Dreamy look*) Yep. Face it Tom, we've walked in his
footsteps already, when we visited his Oklahoma home.

TOM

Not really. Remember, the house was moved because of a
new dam that was built. So he never trod that ground.

GEORGE

The house was the same. Trod his house.

TOM

Too right – his footsteps.

Both gaze into the distance. Sigh.

GEORGE

Let' get started, then. Our new job awaits. (*Sits with tiny hat on, one arm in shirt and swinging lasso*)

TOM

This won't work? Fact: You're no cowboy, <u>George</u>! He not only looked <u>like</u> one, one doing unbelievable rope tricks, he <u>was</u> a cowboy.

GEORGE

I'll be an urban cowboy! Ta. Daa. (*Stands up with outstretched arms in his outfit*)

TOM

Ha! A Looney Toon one maybe.

GEORGE

Toonsville, it might be, but one where your blackouts, flashbacks and semi–comatose states could be an asset. Huh? Think on it.

TOM

Stop it! I'm enough of a cartoon. Be serious and get to the want ads. We have enough jerk commentators. (*Chuckles and points*) That outfit looks stupid.

GEORGE

Great! Humor germinates. Blooms. Do I read ads for dot coms where you can make 5–10–15 thousand dollars a month, or about Quakers?

TOM

Don't be dumb.

GEORGE

OK, Quakers. God, listen to this –.

                    TOM

Incoming. (*Ducks under table, then sits up and just
stares.*)

                    GEORGE

(*Looks at watch, counts down after a short time*) 5–4–3–
2–1

                    TOM

Whoo!

                    GEORGE

Back? OK, listen. I quote, "We <u>had</u> to wire tap the
Quakers for their anti–war doctrines and possible terrorist
tendencies." End quote. NSA. (*Looks up from paper
dumbfounded*)

                    TOM

I may be slow at times, but haven't Quakers been against
war since the 15–1600's?

                    GEORGE

Yep. Talk about oxymoron. This ranks with the ultimate
ones. Don't it? Willie R. bait?

                    TOM

Probably proposed by a moron inhaling too much oxygen.

                    GEORGE

Is this stuff funny? The new Will should be funny like
the old one. Shouldn't he?

                    TOM

I don't know – this stuff's almost too dumb to be funny –
if possible.

GEORGE

This shirt won't work. Restricts my delivery style.

TOM

What style? (*Goes in comatose state again without moving*)

GEORGE

Can't stay – (*Sees Tom, and waits until Tom's normal again*) 3, 2, 1 – was saying, can't be a kid again.

TOM

I don't know.

GEORGE

Wait. Yes, that might do. (*Runs to closet and pulls out a disco shirt – holds up in air*) Disco cowboy! (*Puts on shirt with small hat and lasso*) Rhinestone cowpoke. Disco Pete!

TOM

(*Laughing*) In you're grave. Back to the job ads. (*Freezes again without moving*)

GEORGE

(*Goes over and washes some pots and pans, moves stuff around and waits awhile*) Tommy, Tommy, Tommy. We'll never get this act going at this rate. (*Yells like ghost call*) Tooommmmmmmyy. Where – are you?

TOM

(*Comes out of it*) Whooo, Yikes – Semper Fi. That reminds me, look at this letter label, advertisement. Came other day. Rawley, NC. R–A–W–L–E–Y. Outsourcing has its flaws, it seems.

GEORGE

Guess they never heard of Sir Walter, wherever they're from. (*Takes deep breath*) What about this act?

TOM

No, let's finish the Monopoly game.

GEORGE

(*Jumps up and paces*) I can't. Let's get to the act. Whaddaya say? Huh? Come on!

TOM

May as well, I can't see me winning the way you play. Cheat.

GEORGE

(*Gets hat, disco shirt, lasso*) Good. How about appearance? As I recall, he looked like a nice, shy guy you could trust, or a common sense–type guy. Well, hell, that's me all over.

TOM

(*Laughing*) Hilarious, that self analysis is. Don't look in many mirrors, do you?

GEORGE

Come on, Tom!

TOM

OK. OK. Well, his hat was pushed to the back of his head. (*George pushes hat back, it falls off*) He chewed a lot of gum, hair brushed over forehead in disarray, a little. (*George chews, brushes hair around*) Little more hair. Grins. (*George grins*) <u>Humongous</u> grin. (*George smiles very wide*) Also, had a twinkle in his eye.

GEORGE
How the hell do I do that?

TOM
Fake it!

George looks at audience, grins and does some facial gestures.

Not bad, starting to look like the old films we saw.

GEORGE
(George walks around grinning and scratching head – hat keeps falling off. Picks up hat) Don't remember this part. The hat that is. Falling.

TOM
Maybe we could staple it on.

George stops and stares at Tom.

Now, waddle like a duck. (Laughs)

George duck walks.

OK. Now the lasso, spin it. Let dangle when you read.

George spins, dangles lasso, walks properly, grins, scratches, chews,etc. Occasionally looks at the audience after awhile.

Spooky. Think you almost got it. Could fool me.

GEORGE
That's not much encouragement.

TOM
Great. Now, get a paper and do something funny.

GEORGE

No pressure there.

TOM

No, no. How about – do what did in the bar the other
night, but in character.

GEORGE

(*Gets paper and practices walk, etc, clears throat*)
Listenin' to our executive branch now – and they call me
a humorist (*hee–hee–hee*) ah–ah – well – he's the
kingfish humorist – anyway, what was I saying, let me
see – oh yea – the Attorney General, our A.G. that is –
don't want him gettin' mad at me now (*ha–ha–ha*) no
way– OK –yea– understand – well, anyway, has some
new American idea on torture – .

TOM

(*Breaking in on George*) Not that one. The one about
the church.

GEORGE

Lost me. Never talked about a church.

TOM

You know, the President's one.

GEORGE

Give me strength. You mean about the Unitarian
Executive?

TOM

Yea.

GEORGE

(*Looks at audience, chews gum vigorously, grins and
walks to start up again; e.g. does Will's antics*) Aaaahh–

read here in the paper the President (ha–ha–ha) aah–aah
– that's some polecat we got up there now, ain't it (*hee–
hee–hee*) now don't – please – don't get me wrong – I
like the good old boy –yeap – ahuh – yes I do – met him
onced – liked him, but yea know you gatta watch out for
them Texas boys. (*Pause*) Or is it Massichootit? Who
knows? Ah (*hee–hee–hee*) what was I talking about –a–
a–a–oh yea– said during time of war, – and this seems to
be set up as a never endin' war, now don't it? Well
during time of war our prez – e– dent has expanded new
powers (*hee–hee–hee*) during time of war, yes sirree – he
says con–sti–tu–tion says it – yep it's right in there, even
though no one ever found it before (*hee–hee–hee*) ah–
ah. Calls it unity, universal – what was that now –ah–ah
ah yea Unitarian Executive. That's right – hum – well –
ah–ah– seems to me I smell some limburger here, (*ha–
ha–ha*) yes I do.

TOM

The pilot? Don't get it.

GEORGE

(*Ignores Tom and shrugs shoulders. Exaggerates
Oklahoma country accent*) This here ar–ti–cle further
says – let me see – what did it say – ah–ah– it was a
switched around some how –ah–ah something about
Presidents don't <u>need</u> to follow the law. Says, helps
protect people better. Nice of him, but ah–ah I guess all
the humorists aren't in Congress (*hee–hee–hee*) but the
citizens do appreciate it –ah–ah–ah at least until he
breaks the law on them.

TOM

He's above the law? Not right. (*Dives under kitchen
table and freezes*)

GEORGE

(*Waits awhile*) 3–2–1.

After Tom comes out of his episode and back to normal, George continues as Will Rogers.

GEORGE

Guess it means (*ha–ha–ha*) people <u>like you</u> goes straight to jail. (*Ha–ha–ha*) Do not pass go, ah–ah–(*hee–hee–hee*) you're a security risk and it's OK to just jail you.

TOM

Against my rights! Can't!

GEORGE

Unitarian executive – a–hum–ah–ah – does seem (*hee–hee–hee*) ah–ah war <u>is</u> hell.

TOM

Twaddle, that's what it is. Twaddle! I fought for my rights. Did he? Piffle!!

GEORGE

(*Slumps out of character, looks at Tom*) Huh? Piffle? (*Shakes head and gets back into the Will Rogers character*) Further, it says in this here noooospaper – a unitarian executive means – <u>all powerful</u> – a–a–a– <u>all over</u> world and–and – <u>forever</u>. Dad gum don't that beat all – know what I mean – the whole thing in a nutshell ah–ah– as I ah–ah see it is (*hee–hee–hee*) seems we've created a World Emperor! And it's right there –ah–ah in our –ah–ah constitution. (*Stares at audience, grins, chews hard, grins bigger, then goes and slumps in a chair*)

TOM

(*Laughing*) That was kinda funny. Damn. It might work. Yes, it might. That was funny … wasn't it?

GEORGE

Not really. Maybe. Depressing. Needs work. Need to sneak up on the audience more.

TOM

Whatever.

GEORGE

More Monopoly?

TOM

Seems wrong. Nation of laws. Just men, without them. Gangs. Not a nation. <u>Got</u> to obey laws. <u>Everyone</u>. I – (*Freezes, trance like, speaks without moving, George busies himself*) Incoming, God its dark. Lights all around us. How many? Up in the tree. Get him. Incoming.

Silence.

GEORGE

3–2–1.

TOM

– think it's insane.

GEORGE

(*Weakly says*) Monopoly?

TOM

No! Don't stop! Do another. Our country does need us. Face it, no one really does do common sense, for both sides.

GEORGE

(*Slowly gets out of chair*) Making this stuff funny is hard. Yes sirrryee. And being non–offensive is even harder. Will was something else.

TOM

You need to work on your face.

GEORGE

Sorry, but I'm stuck with it.

TOM

Try to look more – shy like. You know, innocent. No –
impish. That's it! Impish.

GEORGE

(*Tries impish, boyish look – tries it on the audience*)
Right.

*George walks with fake lasso, pretends to do rope tricks. Grins,
chews gum, tries impish, etc. Finally, with head down, glances up
at audience, like he and they know something no one else does.
Grins – wiggles lasso parallel to ground and starts. Continues
Will's antics as talks.*

Anyway – so – ah–ah–well–anyhow at it again (*ha–ha–
ha*) definitions seem to perplex our boys in the White
House (*hee–hee–hee*) all I know is what I read in the
papers (*ha–ha–ha*) yea – it's like you know –a–a–a–one
dose of medicine can save a person's life –and–and– the
same dose –ah–ah– well, it could kill someone else – now
that's a fact. Anyhow –ah–ah–what was I talking –ah–ah
oh yea – paper said our President said we don't torture
prisoners (*hee–hee–hee*) then said, yes he did say –
honest Injin – it said, but we don't rule nothing out to
protect Americans (*ha–ha–ha*) ah–ah– now that's some
plan –ah–ah– remember (*hee–hee–hee*) a plan is nothin'
but a pipe dream (*ha–ha–ha*) even if it becomes a bill –
know what I mean – ah–ah– what was I talking about
again –ah–ah think I have halfzheimers ah–ah yea –
torture – the President's coyotes (*ha–ha–ha*) even
defined it for us (*hee–hee–hee*) ah – now get this –

torture is organ damage leading to death (*hee–hee–hee*)
told my wife I don't torture. (*Giggles*) Even though she
claims I've been a torture our whole marriage (*hee–hee–
hee*) where was I –ah–ah sure glad the good old U.S. of
A. don't torture –ah–ah – or do I smell that limburger
again (*hee–hee–hee*) ah– then that old noooospaper said
over 100 torture deaths in Aah–boo–gravy and black hole
prisons. Doggies –ah–ah–double doggies. Back to the
futures ah–ah– as my ancestors would say. *(As says
'double doggies,' holds lasso parallel to ground and lasso
wilts in middle and loop end goes to ground so looks like
an un–erect penis. Note to director: Trick lasso are
available.)*

TOM

(*Jumps up from listening*) No way! Not right!
Americans don't torture. Period. (*Calms down some*)
Well, anyway, <u>we</u> need to work on funny, George. This
isn't funny. Let's practice our – (*Tom is motionless
again, statue in place a few seconds*) – our skit some
more.

GEORGE

Nope. Realize, can't do it.

TOM

Loser! Elbee, Virgina Woolf guy, would be disappointed.

GEORGE

So, I fail at plays, too.

TOM

Can't, it's all that's left for your career. Like he said
about himself, you've already failed at novels, short
stories, essays and poetry. What's left? Your hero says –
<u>dialogue</u>. Remember his seminar? Let's get going.

GEORGE

Right, Einstein.

TOM

(*Gets paper and sits at table to study*) Let's get some
ideas. I'll read, you figure out how fits – funny stuff.

GEORGE

Give me the easy part, huh?

TOM

Here's one. About welfare. Tough love. Wants to stop
all welfare programs, so people have <u>nothing</u> and thus are
forced to work and be successful. <u>Tough</u> <u>love</u>. Could that
be funny?

GEORGE

I guess, depends how you define torture.

TOM

That's good! Really good. See, this does help.

GEORGE

Nuts! One of us is.

*While Tom talks and reads, George goes to closet and pulls out
toy cowboy guns and holster, stick horse, saddle bags. George puts
on guns; takes stick horse and introduces, silently, to audience.
Makes stick horse bow, rear up, count to 3, gets on and rides, does
trick shooting, quick draw, drops guns, and lassoes stuff, etc. Puts
saddle on back horse, but falls off.*

TOM

Great! Now we're getting somewhere. Should we be
writing this down?

GEORGE

Aaah – not just yet.

TOM

Wooo–whoo whoo hoo? (*Keeps saying it faster as do more woo, woos and gets excited*) How's this, we suggest a piss–up economic policy instead of a trickle–down one.

GEORGE

Daaammmnnn, I repeat, dammnn.

TOM

Yea, yea! Sheesh, why didn't anyone think of this before?

George does Rogers antics while Tom talks.

TOM

Look, <u>super</u> rich pay no tax now. OK, OK maybe yacht sales tax, but no income tax. Don't work, thus, no income. So, we propose, the <u>only</u> <u>taxes</u> levied will be on dividends, capital gains and inheritances, but only inheritances over 4 million dollars. Wow! What a concept. The little people will have money to piss–up with. No more trickling.

GEORGE

Funny too – especially watching all the millionaire senators laughing at it – I can see it now – received your bill proposal and are giving it serious consideration – ha, ha, ha – the uproar would probably knock the damn capital dome off. (*Acts out dramatically*)

TOM

Great! So, it is grist for our mill? Funny?

GEORGE

(*Turns to audience and grins big*) Shucks. (*Acts hicky,*

shy)

                    TOM
Well, maybe not <u>but</u> – (*Freezes again – pauses without moving – yells*) – like thunder and lightnin', people are frightenin'. (*Becomes silent*)

                    GEORGE
God! Poetry during flashbacks. What's next? 3–2–1.

                    TOM
– let's try another tack.

                    GEORGE
(*Slumps in chair*) I'm game.

                    TOM
How about – yes – yea – how about we try to interpret what politicians are really saying?

                    GEORGE
(*Laughs inappropriately*) You <u>are</u> a sadist. Gobblygook is gobblygook. But on the other hand, can't be worse than genital economics.

                    TOM
(*Picks up paper, walks around*) Here's one, new congressional ethics rules. (*Starts laughing or giggling to self*) Ethics and congressional. Same sentence. God, what a joke.

                    GEORGE
What's it say?

                    TOM
Damn, this is stupid. Or they think we are.

GEORGE

They know we are! Time – the great stupefier.
Alzheimer's – the epidemic of politics.

TOM

New rule, listen: You <u>can't</u> take gifts of any kind like
dinner, golf outings, skyboxes, opera tickets. – <u>None</u> –
<u>Zero</u> – <u>Zilch</u> – <u>Period</u>! <u>Unless, unless</u> – you're given', a
campaign contribution along with it. Where's the ethics?
As the old lady said.

GEORGE

Loopholes, loopholes, loopholes! Can they ever "just say,
<u>no</u>." They think it works for drugs and sex, why the hell
not for them?

TOM

Stupid?! No, I guess, only greedy. Loopholes are their
life vein.

GEORGE

Not bad, Tom. Maybe you should be Will.

TOM

No. (*Chuckles*) I might sto – (*Freezes*)

GEORGE

3–2–1

TOM

– stop in the middle of the act, then what?

GEORGE

But it might add suspense. Never know. Suspense can be
good.

TOM

But not very funny.

GEORGE

You know, Tom –

TOM

Yes, I know him.

GEORGE

– eeerrh! Be serious a minute. Your whatever we call
them – episodes, blackouts, seem to be increasing. Think
you should go to the VA for a check up?

TOM

Naw. I'm cured, remember? Don't have to. I guess
ethics is out, not conducive to levity in the vernacular.

GEORGE

Huh? (*Pauses*) Wait, my memory, something's coming —
into it, I can feel it. (*Jumps up, gets into Will Rogers'
character. Looks at audience*) Howdy folks (*ha–ha–ha*)
now I know ah–ah I made some fine – yes fine speeches,
even hit (*hee–hee–hee*) on a bright idea now and again,
but what I –ah–ah– talk –ah–ah– talk over with you birds
can't –dah– compete with Congress – no sir, them
polecats – in Congress that is – well –ah–ah they're like
children that never growed up (*ha–ha–ha*) and –and–
well, what was I gonna talk about here now –ah–ah–
awful lot more said on both sides of Congress and ah and
both sides that don't know nothing (*hee–hee–hee*) well,
ah–ah.

TOM

What's the point here, George? Not getting it.

GEORGE

(*Still as Rogers*) Well, anyway –ah– as I was sayin' ah–ah
all Prez–e–ents have one –ah–yes–ah–yes, one thing in
common, that's for sure. (*Ha–ha–ha*) No, no it's –ah–not
what your thinkin' ah–ah nope. Naw, naw, (*ha–ha–ha*)
no sex talk here folks and ah no–no–no (*hee–hee–hee*)
anyway, we don't torture, remember. Well, (*ha–ha–ha*)
I've noted Prez–e–dents tout about peace. Ah–ah–ah
peace this, and peace that ah–ah peace everywhere –

TOM

Good one, George. Remember Nixon – Vietnam's goal:
"lasting peace," he touted.

GEORGE

Then –ah–ah– now don't misunderstand me, they're all
good men – honorable. I know most of them, but take
Johnson (*Acts like on soap box*) "Our one desire, one
determination, commitment is to peace" or some such –
ah–ah– and Bush, Sr. (*hee–hee–hee*), he tickled me. A
fine man though – anyway (*hee–hee–hee*) said, "I hate
war. I love peace." (*hee–hee–hee*) then invaded Panama
or some such place. Or –or – that Clinton feller, another
fine man. But his eupi – euphonics –ah–ah euphemisms
stopped me dead. Talked peace, but –ah–ah– but, but no
one could understand him. Ask 'em in Yugoslavia or–or
whatever it's called now. He euphemismed them into 4
or 5 countries. Now – now – that's what I call peace talks
(*ha–ha–ha*) ah–ah–wh'd that Prussian von somebody say
–yea–ah–you know –ah – 200 years ago (*hee–hee–hee*) 'a
conqueror is always a lover of peace' – yep that was it.
Wonder if that covey in Washington knows that.

TOM

You need to juice that up some. Like – get in something
like – Clinton never could define is – peace is war. Get
it?

GEORGE

(*Stares at Tom, then audience, jumps on horse*) Riding
clears my head.

TOM

How about this (*Reading paper*) – says, due to Freedom
of – (*Freezes, recites in monotone voice*)
>   Cannons to right of them.
>   Cannons to left of them,
>   Boldly they rode and well
>   Into the mouth of hell,
>   What a waste, we learned our lesson not.

(*Comes out of episode*) – Freedom of Information Act,
documents surrounding the Tonkin Gulf Resolution are
public.

GEORGE

(*Scratches head and crotch*) Yea, but who cares now?
Old news.

TOM

(*Holds up a paper*) God, do you believe this?

GEORGE

Don't know, can't see it from here.

TOM

(*Reading, pointing at paper excitedly*) Stevenson, U.N.
Ambassador said – if the U.N. is going to be relevant, it
must take a firm stand – without doubt the North
Vietnamese government had been guilty of planned
deliberate aggression, military action.

GEORGE

Sounds just like when they justified President Jr's I–Rack
pre–emptive strike.

TOM

Better yet – listen here now – says –, documents show
Stevenson's proclamations were based on <u>lies</u>. Lies, do
you believe it – <u>lies</u>. Boat attacks in Tonkin never
happened. Damn. All made up.

GEORGE

Yep. Our general fudged, exaggerated and concocted,
too. Definitely bait for Willie R. (*Smiles, chews gum,
cocks head*) Knowed that vial of anthrax and those
diagrams weren't right – but <u>did</u> guarantee peace by
conquest!

TOM

All my problems – (*Freezes, quiet pause then says without
moving, in a monotone voice*) What is the sound of one
hand clapping? (*Pauses, yells*) Nature! (*Pauses –
unfreezes*) – problems were avoidable!

GEORGE

Know what you're saying?

TOM

Yea! My life's pissed for nothing.

GEORGE

Not that, your poetry or whatever.

TOM

What? Don't know what you're talking about. Damn
them. All unnecessary. A waste, meaningless.

GEORGE

No! Stop it! You were honorable. Heroic. Courageous.
Fought for truth as knew it. Valiant. Can't take that
away. Mirrors don't crack when you peer at them. As
the saying goes – your OK, they're not OK.

TOM

Damn, damn – Damn.

GEORGE

Don't get these poems, sayings, from your black hole –
not quite right somehow.

TOM

What sayings?

GEORGE

(*Said dejectedly*) Forget it. The cannons are booming.
Left and right. Can the Fatherland be far behind the
Homeland? Yea, Unitarian.

TOM

Where'd that come from? Skip the church thing. Now
what?

GEORGE

(*Walks like Will Rogers to get into character, uses props,
stares at audience, chews gum.*) (*Hee–hee–hee*) Seems to
me, ah–ah– if you ask ah–ah– , and no one rarely does,
but anyway, seems to me it's hard for U.S. citizens, press
(*Pauses*) – Americans! Any how, it's hard –ah– really
hard for us to believe our President would <u>lie</u> to us. But
does! All do – did – whatever –even if it's mostly by
omission. Yep, Prez –e – dents lie.

TOM

Sheesh, here's another one. Keeps getting better. Who
said this?

GEORGE

Can see the lie bit worked. Sheesh, yourself.

TOM

(*Reading, paying no attention to George*) Listen: I have
not, and do not, intend to announce the timetable of our
program. – the rate of withdrawal will depend on
developments on the ground – this will be the greatest
progress since World War II towards lasting world peace.
Well, who said it? (*Looks up*)

GEORGE

President Jr., says that at all his fund raisers.

TOM

Boop! Nixon. "69" speech. Basically meant – (*Freezes
again without moving, says in monotone voice:*)
　　To see the world in a grain of sand,
　　And heaven in a wild flower
　　Hold infinity in the palm of our hand,
　　Thou art the food of worms.

GEORGE

3–2–1.

TOM

(*Unfreezes*) – Meant none of the public's damn business.
Piss off. That was his point.

GEORGE

Damn. Now, <u>that</u> poem really sounded familiar. Blake?
Mix of two?

TOM

Huh? (*Holds head in bewilderment*) How about a beer?
A bar break seems called for.

GEORGE

Do seem to be going nowhere.

TOM

Yes we are! Damn, I'm the one that's supposed to be
depressed. So, get off it George.

GEORGE

Do you even remember your poems? (*Pauses with no
answer*) Oh well. Hey! Why not try it tonight?

TOM

Yea, a drink – we try it every night – clears our heads.

GEORGE

No. No. It's a great idea. Let's take the act on the road.
Now!

TOM

Tonight?

GEORGE

Why not?

TOM

(*Thinks*) Why not?

Tom and George pick up props – saddle bag, hat, horse and guns.

TOM

This could be just what the skit doctor ordered.

GEORGE

A needed shot in the arm.

Both slam way out the door.

*After a momentary pause, someone (audience person, stage
manager personnel, anyone) walks across front of stage (like in old
time boxing matches) holding up large card that says: " Hours*

have passed"

After cardholder is off stage and a short pause, George and Tom burst through door –their clothes tattered, black eyes and in general disarray. George falls onto the floor with props he's carrying, scattering. Tom plops on a couch/pull out bed. Both are laughing.

GEORGE

(*From the floor, laughing louder and louder*) That was great! Really great. Did you see McFearson slide down the length of that bar?

TOM

(*Holding belly laughing*) And plop off the end into the garbage can!

GEORGE

Yea. (*Laughing uncontrolled*) Legs flailing. Stuck! Upside down!

TOM

Should be called McSon, no fear.

GEORGE

What a donnybrook. It's been years. Why don't we do that more often?

TOM

One guess. Look at us.

GEORGE

(*Laughing subsides some, walking around by now*) Enough fun. Let's see if we can improve our act now.

TOM

(*Look at each other in silence, then both burst out*

laughing, rolling around) That was too much.

GEORGE

God, it was funny. But it wouldn't work. (*Still giggling*)
Groucho Rogers, the fifth Marx brother.

TOM

Those little legs on the stick horse. Walking around like
Groucho, cigar smoking. (*Does Groucho antics*) And
you kept pulling the hat off, looking at it like one of you
were lost. (*Pauses*) Yea, alright. Maybe it was just the
booze.

GEORGE

Well, what did we learn? (*Pauses)*

TOM

I don't black out when I drink?

Both look at each other in silence.

GEORGE

Weird. Treatment?

TOM

Don't I wish. If I wasn't cured, I'd suggest that treatment
to the VA people. Also learned, it's probably not a good
idea to do political jokes in front of a bunch of drunks.

GEORGE

Ha! Learn? I learned – should probably adopt the views
of moral drunks. I'm not too pretty to start with.

TOM

No! Hecklers – you need to learn how to handle then.
Kicking, spitting, swearing didn't seem to work. Now,
did it?

GEORGE

How?

TOM

Show respect to the President.

GEORGE

Isn't that the point of our act? No respect.

TOM

Not really. It's not him. He's irrelevant. Stick to policy name calling. Nothing personal, as they say.

GEORGE

Even if he's spoiled.

TOM

Maybe, I don't know. Consider – taking the heckler's point of view and work backwards.

GEORGE

(*Grins like Will Rogers at audience*) You say To–mah–to, I say To–may–to. You say terrorist surveillance. I say domestic spying.

TOM

Kind of. Try harder.

GEORGE

Huh? (*Looks confused*) This is hard. You mean, maybe, I shouldn't call Mr. President a liar? At least not outright.

TOM

There yea go. (*Pauses*) Hint, that maybe he misinterpreted CIA data that was 95% certain there were no WMDs. And ask whether a 5% chance was enough to go to war on. Ask the "patriot" – (*Give hand sign for quotation mark*) his thoughts on that!

GEORGE

You're kidding, right? Ask? I wouldn't be worth that plug nickel cowboys always talked about.

TOM

(*Said slowly, contemptuously*) See what you mean. Reason, logic have limits with the obstructive righteous.

GEORGE

Face it, this President's truth is Pinocchio–esque.

TOM

Yea, they sure have this PR, Madison Avenue stuff down. But good. Twist anything into something else. Disorientating.

GEORGE

Heroes to bums. Bums to heroes. Swift boats. Sounds like a board game. Facts – fooyie.

TOM

Now what?

GEORGE

Only play for drunks? Or do we try harder on a real Will?

TOM

But Groucho was cool! (*Whines*) Please can we have – Groucho? Will Groucho Marx Rogers has a nice ring.

GEORGE

(*Laughing*) Of a cracked Liberty Bell. Not the ring of a Monastic ethereal one. Marx is for a bar, we want class.

TOM

Class?

GEORGE

Cowboy, hicky class. Not no class. Now the plot.

TOM

Huh? Plot! We don't have a plot. War maybe. Saving
our democracy, maybe. What? Plot? I'm – (*Freezes like
a statue again and speaks without moving, in a monotone
tone*)
    What everyone knows, I know
    What I know, I alone know
    When a fish swims, water is muddied –

GEORGE

3–2–1.

TOM

(*Comes out of it and finishes sentence*) I'm lost!

GEORGE

Forget it. The sketch, my kingdom for a sketch. As
Dickie III said.

TOM

Stupider and stupider. Maybe we should leave politics.
How about the economy?

GEORGE

Isn't that mostly government, politics?

TOM

Don't be stupid, too!

GEORGE

Back off. I'm thinking now – I'm all think! Question –

why do you believe so many Senators are millionaires?

TOM

Good businessmen? (*Shrugs*) Born that way?

GEORGE

No to the first. Some, few to the second. Corporation
business is government now. So, mostly they've legalized
bribery, blackmail, kickbacks – call it legislation. Use
fact finding excursions, earmarking, fundraising as tactics.
To create their own personal money non–market
accounts. Clearly, the bank robbers are in charge of the
bank. Seems should share wealth, but they just don't. So
much for bible advice.

TOM

Whatever. Think it might be funny? Seemed boring to
me. Well, try one – with your outfit on and all – go on,
try one.

GEORGE

(*Walks around and* acts *up in Will Rogers character*)
Let's see. Aaahh?

TOM

Outsourcing could be something. Seen that Dobbs guy,
CNN, who seems to get laughs on it. Come on.

*George fumbling through papers looking for ideas. Tom picks up a
book and leafs through it.*

Try something. Come on. <u>Why not</u> try the outsourcing?

GEORGE

(*Twirls lasso, Will Rogers walk, gum chewing, shy look
etc. at audience e.g. does all Rogers antics as talks*) Ah–
like I say –ah– all I know is what I read in the papers –ah

(*ha–ha–ha*) guess that's not much (*hee–hee–hee*) –ah–
not, now that I think about it (*ha–ha–ha*) anyhow, take
this outsourcing –ah–yea–ah– seems cockeyed to me –ah
(*ha–ha–ha*) not sure what it is –ah– ah– this outsourcing,
but –yes–ah – but seems we should want more jobs –ah–
here! Bankers are all for it, outsourcing, –ah–so–so know
must be somethin' wrong (*hee–hee–hee*) well, as I said, –
ah–ah– people don't want charity –ah–ah– want a job,
not to starve, health care. Seems to me–a yea– yes it does
–ah–ah– it's all cockeyed. Take –ah the wealth of all
these billionaires today ah–ah– well ah– I bet the people
without now, contributed –ah–ah– in someway somehow
to that wealth. Outsourcing like –ah (*ha–ha–ha*) –ah
seems like more perspiration than common sense. Now
don't – ah–get me wrong, competing for jobs is good –ah
(*hee–hee–hee*) even if thousands of miles away –ah–ah–
fair. Shucks don't scare me none. But –ah– but it takes
away the Great Depression gains –ah–ah–yea– you know
– benefits– don't seem right no how. So –ah– this here
outsourcing –ah–ah– why, it's not competition –or–or–
fair or–or–or helpful to any workers –ah–ah foreign or
domestic. Seems to me –ah–ah– now I'm not good with
words –ha–ha – that's why they call me a humorist –ah
(*hee–hee–hee*) well my word would be ex–ploy–ta–tion.
Yep, dad gum –ah– if it don't sound –ah– like, in simple
human terms –ah (*ha–ha–ha*) –ah it sounds like just
screw the workers – sure does – you know – cockeyed.
Ah–ah sure no small step for –ah–ah– mankind, as
someone said. Only a giant leap for –ah–ah– for cor–
por–a–tions. That's –ah– what it says to me. Ah– an –
ah– outrage –ah– yes–outrage– by the populace seems
reasonable. (*Stops acting, goes over to Tom who is
leafing through a book*) Well, what do you think? If I
get the mannerisms right, like are in my head, it seems
funny.

TOM

Don't think he'd say "screw." Now, how do we empty
your head, get it out, so it works.

GEORGE

Come on, help me.

TOM

I don't know. Try another, I'll watch closer, give an
honest critique. OK? (*Starts leafing through book again,
as George gets in character*)

GEORGE

(*Twirls lasso etc again, quickly looks at newspaper,
thinks, then starts*) Says here –ah–ah– in this
nooospaper –ah – this Darwin (*ha–ha–ha*), monkey guy –
now don't that beat all – Washington's full of monkeys –
evolution's top branch – anyway –ah–ah says Darwin was
a student of Adam Smith –ah–(*ha–ha–ha*) and, Darwin
felt species evolved like manufacturers evolved products.
Ah–ah– that seems sort of funny (*ha–ha–ha*). Dang, I
knowed our species evolved from a committee proposal.
Well now, I wonder –ah–ah is that how Ford got an
Edsel? The car, not the boy (*ha–ha–ha*) you younguns
may not get that one. Ah–ah– anyhow –ah– does sound
like man's headed for a massive ecological collapse. (*Out
of character, asks Tom*)
Well? – Well?

TOM

Almost.

GEORGE

Almost what? Bad acting? Bad delivery? Bad topic?
Too intellectual? Too stupid?

TOM

Yes. (*Throws book leafing through on table*)

GEORGE

(*With paper again*) Encouragement would help, <u>Tom</u>.
Here, yes, here, listen. They're trying to <u>legalize lying</u>.

TOM

What? (*Pauses*) Holy hell. (*Jumps up, goes back to book
and leafs through book*) Just had a brilliant epiphany.

GEORGE

What other kinds are there? – So, I guess your lack of
interest is saying: don't want to hear how an <u>FCC
declared</u> prohibition, not being a <u>law, rule or regulation</u>,
allows T.V. news to be fabricated – OK? At least, Jr.'s
court ruled that way.

TOM

No. Here – the book – our answer – could work.

GEORGE

I'm all ears; what? (*Said slowly, despondent, hurt
feelings*)

TOM

<u>Act</u> like Will Rogers, yes, but use <u>his</u> <u>exact</u> words!
<u>Exactly</u> as he did! Forget yours.

GEORGE

Isn't that plagiarism or something? We'd be no better
than congressmen.

TOM

Not really. I don't think. Anyway, this book – (*Holds
book up*) has his quotes, speeches, letters, articles.

GEORGE

Still, doesn't sound right.

TOM

(*Reads from book*) Listen to this one, could have been
written today; I quote: "The Democrats will agree to
peddle Texas, and I am certain the Republicans will let
Massachusetts go." Talk about double entendre –
Bush/Kerry all over again. His stuff's still relevant!

GEORGE

Geez. Things never change. Maybe there is a string
puller, King, behind the powers that be. We just don't
know who the King is. Do we?

TOM

Back to earth, George. This has promise – definitely
could work. Listen to these, then try one yourself.

GEORGE

Is this public domain stuff?

TOM

Stop crying and listen.

GEORGE

Where are your blackouts? When need one?

TOM

Who cares? Listen: the American people would trade 10
investigations for one conviction. Great, isn't it?
Germaine!

GEORGE

I didn't laugh.

TOM

You said it wrong. It's not what you say, it's how you say it.

GEORGE

What?! You said it. I didn't laugh.

TOM

George, join in or you'll never get it. Here's another one: Imagine a Congress that squanders billions trying to find out where some candidate spent a few thousand! God! Ethics, campaign reform, lobbying, they're still tackling the same stuff.

GEORGE

Don't need to plagiarize, I could come up with one of these, like: All the money spent on government, and it's not one bit better than what we got 20 years ago for 1/3 the price.

TOM

Got it! He said same thing. You're good. Tackle issues, not people.

GEORGE

Get out. Will said that? But, where's the humor?

TOM

Try this for pertinence: When you get into trouble 5000 miles from home, we've got to have been looking for it. God – Iraq ring a bell? What insight. Or this: They keep juggling millions and we owe billions.

GEORGE

So, deficit spending's not new. Let me try one. (*While looking at book, gets into character. Smiles at audience while twirling lasso and doing Will's antics as talk*) Well,

lets ah–ah see now –ah– well I'm always writin' about
politics, Supreme Court, World Court, disarmament, any,
yes any and everything. (*Ha–ha–ha*) –ah–ah– but you
know, I don't know any more about 'em than a boweavil
– (*ha–ha–ha*) and –an– I don't even know how to spell
boll weevil. But have a sprinkling of knowledge on one
thing. The difference between good times and bad times,
a–huh–ah– an it's gasoline, and what goes with it.
Gasoline was never much higher. A few men – yep – just
a few it seems and –ah–an they see price is kept up. It's
not regulated by supply and demand, it's regulated by
manipulation. (*Smiles. Comes out of character, looks at
book*) Hard to believe, ain't it? How long ago was this
written – what, 1920's?

TOM

Not bad, not – (*Freezes again and recites, motionless,
monotone voice, while George flips through the book to
read next lines*)
    If New and Old, disastrous feud,
    Must ever shock, like armed foes,
    And this be true, till time shall close,
    I must never wear hose –

GEORGE

Tennyson? But why all the screwed up endings? 3–2–1.

TOM

– A – not bad at all. Need to be more Willie like.

GEORGE

Maybe I <u>should</u> just read his stuff. I'm not a good thinker.

TOM

Stinker?

GEORGE

Get your ears checked. Anyway, he's funny, but his stuff
isn't. Face it, I'm not funny.

TOM

Come on; get that shy "aw shucks" look. Remember his
movies? He was cutish. And remember his rule – always
tell the truth. You can exaggerate, but only exaggerate
the truth. But be cute.

GEORGE

(*Laughing*) No way this – (*Points to face*) – can be cute.

TOM

Try it – flirt with people.

George turns to audience and tries.

Do a rope trick with devilish facial expressions.

George tries.

Concentrate – devilish, cute, shy.

George tries all facial things – chuckles little like small boy.

Read the line now. (*Gives George the book*)

GEORGE

(*Grins big*) Elections –ah– you know – them things we
are made to –ah–ah tolerate every four years, elections –
is just what we need. We don't know what we need 'em
for, but –ah–ah it's for something, If only (*ha–ha–ha*) to
get one–half of our folks sore at the other half. (*Stops
and grins at audience*)

TOM

Better, much better.

GEORGE

Disconnect – that's the key. My words <u>should not</u> match
my antics. Yea, disconnect. Key to success.

TOM

You've always been that. Just like any Unitarian
Executive. Disconnected.

GEORGE

Let me try one of mine. On environment maybe. See if I
get his stupid look – serious word – thing.

TOM

It's late. Give it a rest till tomorrow.

GEORGE

Tomorrows never come. Besides, I'm getting it – I think
– reinforcement <u>now</u> would be prudent, to quote an old
President.

TOM

(*Yawns*) Whatever.

GEORGE

(*Rustles through newspaper, stops, reads, gets into
character*) (*Hee–hee–hee*). Now I know –ah– I should
quit jok'n' about these boys –ah –ah– in Wash–ing–ton.
(*Ha–ha–ha*) –ah or they might make a loop –ah–ah
loophole or somethin' out of me – good boys up there
though – know most of em –ah–ah– good people and, –
ah want to do good –yea. Yet, they're at it again. Seems
loopholes must taste good or–or somethin'. Know what I
mean. I'm only –ah–ah– an amateur humorist compared
to them boys and girls (*ha–ha–ha*) –yes–sir –ah–ah – I

make a joke, don't hurt no one, but –ah–but them –ah–
ah–they make a joke and–and– an it becomes a law –
(*hee–hee–hee*) now take the–ah–new Clean Water Act –
shucks, I know they –ah–ah like clean water –ah–yea–<u>me</u>
<u>too</u>! But why –ah–ah– but why take good words like
'mining waste' and the like and –and–ah–an redefine 'em
as 'land fill' (*hee–hee–hee*) guess can blame it on a
committee. Darwin again (*ha–ha–ha*) –ah–ah always
seem obliged to word fiddle up there. Anyway –ah–ah–
what was I sayin' –ah–ah– help me out here – oh–yea
well seems if it's <u>waste</u> –well –ah –can't do nothing with
it! But – un huh – if <u>fill</u>, well –see–if it's called fill – well
can just about dump it anywhere. Like yea–ah–ah like
can dump fill in rivers, ah–ah wetlands, –ah–shucks, can
dump it in any old water. Heck, now that's a ah–that's a
loophole, one of them humongous earth movers could go
through. As I – I –ah – I see it, won't be no water left to
have an act for –ah–ah–clean or otherwise. (*Drops out of
Will Rogers character*) Well? Tom, come on Tom.
Wake up! It wasn't that bad, was it?

TOM
(*Yawning*) Sorry man, I'm tired. What I caught seemed
OK.

GEORGE
(*Opening couch bed as talks*) Just OK. Did you see my
face? Think I got him!

TOM
Lets go to sleep. Try again tomorrow.

GEORGE
(*Puts lights out. Talks in dark*) OK, but are ya sure I
shouldn't try more tonight – think I'm getting it.

TOM

I know, I know, but rest is good. There's time tomorrow.

GEORGE

But is my face working?

TOM

Great. Now, give it a rest. Sleep.

GEORGE

Maybe I should get up and practice looking in a mirror.

TOM

George – <u>Tomorrow</u>! Plenty of time.

GEORGE

I guess, but I hate to stop when I'm so close. My face is getting great.

TOM

<u>I'm</u> – (*Freezes, obvious by silence, speaks in monotone voice*)

    The – <u>sun</u> forgets his course like a drunken man; he hesitates. In vain: he is hurried afar into an unknown Night. (*Silence again*)

GEORGE

Blake, William, –3–2–1 –

TOM

– I'm sure. Plenty of time.

GEORGE

Good night, Tom. (*Silence*) OK, sleep tight, hope dreams don't bite. (*Silence again, all is dark*).

A few seconds pass. Suddenly doors burst open, windows break.

Flashlight beams all around, lights to apartment switch on. 2–3 men in door. Someone looks through windows from fire escape. Some with dark shielded helmet of SWAT team.

MBS–1
Freeze! Hands up. Let's go.

GEORGE
(*Jumps to sitting position, rubbing eyes, Tom still sleeping. Looks at gun, masked men*) What the hell? Take what you want. But we're on the dole, broke, jobless. Have nothing.

MBS–1
Funny. You <u>have</u> a <u>big</u> mouth. The inquisition <u>is</u> here when you need them. (*Laughs evilly*) Get it? <u>Us</u>. And you thought Homeland Security had no sense of humor. (*Laughs falsely again*)

GEORGE
Homeland what? Give me a break. This is America. Not Homeland. Take what the hell you want and piss off. (*Lays back down*)

MBS–2
You terrorists are all alike. Like an egg, tough on the outside, soft in the middle.

GEORGE
(*Sits up again*) Terrorists? Nuts! Need to work on the metaphor, simile, whatever, l–i–t–o–t–e (*said stretched out*) more.

TOM
(*Suddenly jumps up*) Terrorists! Where? (*Looks around, sees a man*) Oh my god, terrorists. (*Points at men*) Why do you want us?

MBS–1

Get dressed, you assholes. (*Pushes both out off bed to floor*)

TOM

Who the hell are you guys? George?

George shrugs.

MBS–2

We're Homeland Security and you two are under arrest as battlefield combatants.

GEORGE

(*Laughing*) Is that all. OK – who sent you guys? Our act tonight wasn't that offensive. To warrant this joke.

TOM

Christ! Look at our window. George, this isn't a joke. Those weapons are real. My army training says – shit.

GEORGE

Wait a minute, there must be a mistake. Got the wrong apartment. Something. We're <u>Americans</u>. Patriotic as the next guy.

MBS–2

Not what we hear. Subversive.

MBS–1

Aiding and abetting also come to mind. Sedition too, if you consider what you said about our President.

TOM

Come on gang. This is silly. We're nowhere near a battlefield.

MBS–2

Everyone is – today; don't kid yourself. Nowhere to hide.
Now, get dressed. Our job is to prevent cells like yours
from acting or hatching their plots. Your part in this war
is over, pal. The shell is cracked and chickens have come
home to roost.

GEORGE

With the eggs again. What's with that? Fetish? What?

MBS–1

Move it. (*Pushes them toward clothes*)

GEORGE

Wait. Wait. (*Pushed again, yells*) <u>Wait</u>! Just one damn
minute. I get a call. I can call my lawyer.

MBS–1

(*Chuckles*) Cute. Don't do that anymore.

GEORGE

What?

MBS–2

You heard him. Constitutional too.

GEORGE

My Constitution gives me the right. I ask for a phone
call, I get one. It's the law!

MBS–1

Our Constitution trumps yours. Once declared battle–
field combatants – rules change.

GEORGE

I'm, we're – (*Points to Tom and himself*) bonafide
Americans. The Constitution is the Constitution.

MBS–2

Right! And it says the President has the right to put your
sorry asses in jail, if you're deemed a threat. You are so
deemed and his constitutional right trumps your
constitutional right, so stated by the country's top lawyer,
the Attorney's General, our boss. You can be <u>indefinitely</u>
detained.

GEORGE

We have to be dreaming. (*Knocks Tom on head with
knuckles*)

TOM

Oooow, that hurt.

GEORGE

No dream. OK, how about a lawyer. I still get one of
them.

MBS–2

Nope. Not in your situation. You're in big trouble, fella.
We need inform – <u>no one</u>.

GEORGE

We become missing persons? Permanently?

MBS–1

Not really. Your case will be investigated internally,
<u>secretly</u>, and a decision made <u>in time</u>, as to disposition.
Secretly.

MBS–2

In the meantime, you're off the streets and your terrorist
intentions halted.

MBS–1

It would help your case if you divulged your other cell

members. Show cooperation with the authorities.

TOM
What? We have none. We're none.

MBS–1
That attitude won't help.

TOM
Dear God, give us strength.

GEORGE
I suppose a court hearing in the near future is out of the question, too.

MBS–2
(*Laughing*) Now you're getting the idea. You're in deep shit.

TOM
Are you sure you have the right people? Look at us –do we look like rebels?

MBS–1
Honestly – yes.

TOM
George, think of something!

GEORGE
No phone call, no lawyer, no hearing and I suppose other Bill of Rights points are out, too. Torture? Habeas corpus?

MBS–2
Yep. We're at <u>war</u> son, and being at <u>war</u> means something. Torture's OK, even though we don't do it.

Unless you force us.

GEORGE

Wait, Constitution says – let me get our copy. (*Gets book*) it says –

MBS–2

(*Cuts sentence off*) Doesn't matter – now. (*Takes book and throws it in garbage can*) War's in play, remember.

GEORGE

What? During war we become an emperorship! That was a joke. And face it, this kind of war will last forever. Forever! (*Says forever slowly and loudly*)

MBS–1

Probably, but don't start. Anger will only make your situation worse.

GEORGE AND TOM

How?

GEORGE

Tell me again – how you know it's us. Please. Before the governmental void engulfs us.

MBS–1

Don't have to, but what the heck. Are you boys familiar with Amedeo's Bar?

GEORGE

Yea, drink there all the time.

MBS–2

While there, have you ever inferred the President was a liar?

TOM

Well, he is. And often – WMDs, torture, wire tapping, interrogation techniques, nation building, Medicare personal accounts, Hurricane Katrina efforts, elderly prescription benefits, Saddam and 9–11. Yea, had them in a comedy routine – clowning.

MBS–1

And made reference to the President's looks.

TOM

Said that was a bad idea. That frog face thing. (*Shaking head*)

MBS–2

Suggested he manipulated judges.

MBS–1

Intentionally changed regulations to pollute, helping his CEO buddies?

MBS–2

Said he never balanced a budget, when he claims he has, or that he rigged elections or that his tax breaks only favored the top 1/5 of 1% or –

GEORGE

OK, stop. But that was not said in malice, it was for comic effect. That's what comics do.

TOM

Yea, make fun of leaders. Helps to keep them honest.

GEORGE

We're no more terrorists than you are. We're in no cell.

TOM
Closest to a cell we get is a cellphone.

GEORGE
Yea, free speech is all we were practicing.

MBS–1
Security trumps free speech in time of <u>War</u>. You're guilty
by you own words. You admit it.

MBS–2
National security – most important – this <u>is</u> War.
Without national security, where would <u>we</u> be.

GEORGE
But we're comics – the inquisition's not appropriate for
us.

TOM
Is it for anyone – appropriate?

GEORGE
Guys! <u>Think</u> a little here. Amedeo's is a bar we always
go to – a second home almost. We were telling jokes.
Harmless.

MBS–1
Right. Didn't <u>you</u> start an anti–American riot there
recently? During your recruiting efforts?

MBS–2
And the patrons – the patriotic ones anyway – took
exception and stopped your – terror speak.

TOM
Damn. Did we just time warp to Orwellville?

GEORGE

Couple jokes flopped, that was all. Come on guys.

TOM

No big deal.

MBS–1

Enough bull, let's go. Get dressed, hurry up. (*Gets a little hostile, pushy, fed up*) Face your destiny.

George and Tom put on clothes. George picks up his Rogers' props (especially guns, saddle bag)to put away in the closet. Make prominent at this point.

GEORGE

Is this what your blackouts are like? See weird crap like this?

TOM

No. They're more angelic, peaceful.

MBS–1

Shut up. Too late to talk about peace now. No more talk.

George handling toy gun, and saddle bag, trying to put in closet.

MBS–2

Look out! Has a gun! Bomb! God, looks like a bomb. Drop it!

MBS–1

Drop it, quick.

MBS–2

Last chance.

GEORGE
(*Holds saddle bag up*) It's just a saddle bag prop and
<u>toy</u> –

Shots ring out. George and Tom fall.

MBS–2
(*Checks bodies*) They're both dead.

MBS–1
Damn. Needed their contacts. To catch more of the
cell.

*Stage goes dark – after few seconds hear music from news
broadcast while dark.*

*News – Da da– da– ta– da da. Good morning to all – y'all. Hope
your day's starting out great. Lead story this morning deals with
terror – but good news – late last night a terrorist cell was exposed
– two dead – prevented apartment house from being blown up.
Security's working folks, but don't put your guard down yet. Fear's
not over. Also, stocks are up and guess what star dumped their
spouse. Who woulda thunk?*

Sound fades away –

CURTAIN FALLS

www.ingramcontent.com/pod-product-compliance
Lightning Source LLC
Chambersburg PA
CBHW030529260626
47157CB00005B/1950